Cinderella

illustrated by

Jess Stockham

Child's Play (International) Ltd
Ashworth Rd, Bridgemead, Swindon, SN5 7YD UK
Swindon   Auburn ME   Sydney
© 2011 Child's Play (International) Ltd   Printed in Heshan, China
ISBN 978-1-84643-440-2   L260411CFT06114402
1 3 5 7 9 10 8 6 4 2
www.childs-play.com

Once upon a time, there was a young girl
called Cinderella. She loved her father
dearly, but her stepmother and stepsisters
were very cruel to her.
They made her do all the work around
the home, and sleep on the floor.
Worst of all, she had to wear
dirty old rags instead of proper clothes.

One day, a note arrived from the palace, inviting the family to a ball in honour of the king's son. Cinderella's stepsisters and stepmother spent days talking about what they would wear to the party, but they told Cinderella she could not go.

At last, the day of the ball arrived.
Cinderella helped everyone get ready,
and watched them leave for the palace.

When the house was quiet and empty,
she suddenly felt sad. She sat down
and started to cry.
"I would so love to go to a ball, just once,"
she sniffed.

All of a sudden, there was an enormous bang, and a large woman appeared in a cloud of smoke.

"Hello, Cinders," she smiled.
"I'm your fairy godmother. Don't be sad. Would you like to go to the ball as well?"

When Cinderella nodded, her fairy godmother sprang into action. "Right," she ordered, "Fetch me the biggest pumpkin you can find!"

Cinderella did so at once, without asking why.
Her fairy godmother scooped out all the seeds,
put it on the floor, and hit it with her wand.
Immediately, the pumpkin turned into a fine
coach, decorated with silver and gold.

"Right," said the fairy godmother.
"Now for a little horsepower!"
She pointed her wand at a family
of mice playing in the garden,
and all at once they became
a team of six dappled horses.

"Now, you'll need someone to take you," continued the godmother, turning a family of rats into finely dressed coachmen.

"And of course you can't possibly go to the ball dressed like that!" She lifted her wand again, and Cinderella's rags miraculously turned into the most beautiful outfit of gold and silver, silk and lace.

"Final touch!" said the godmother.
"A girl has to have great shoes!"
Suddenly, there appeared on Cinderella's tiny feet a pair of the most exquisite glass slippers.

"Remember this," said the godmother.
"I cannot keep this magic going for ever.
You must leave the ball before midnight."
Cinderella nodded. "Right! Time to go!
You mustn't be late!"

And Cinderella found herself carried off
to the palace in a flash.

When she arrived, everyone wanted to know who the lovely princess was, with her majestic coach and fine servants.

"What a beautiful girl!" exclaimed the king.
"In such splendid clothes," agreed the queen.
The prince walked right up to her.

"Will you dance with me?" he asked.

"Of course," agreed Cinderella, and the two of them danced all the way around the palace, and back again. They ate the finest food and drank the nicest drinks, and danced some more. They were interested in all the same things, and talked and talked without stopping once.

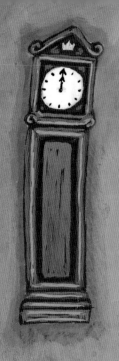

Cinderella was enjoying herself so much,
she forgot to look at the clock all evening.
The clock began to strike midnight.
She remembered her fairy godmother's
warning, but her beautiful
dress was already
starting to fray!

Cinderella screamed,
and ran as fast as she could
out of the ballroom and down
the long corridors towards the palace gates.

When she got there, her clothes were in tatters, and the waiting coach had turned back into a simple pumpkin, surrounded by a noisy pack of mice and rats.

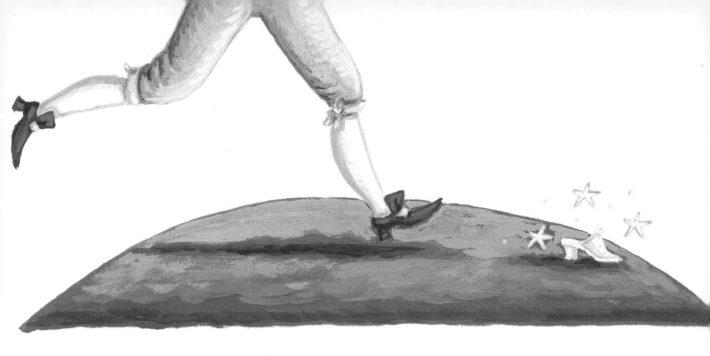

The prince chased Cinderella, but could not keep up.
He stopped at the palace gates to pick up one
of the precious glass shoes that had slipped off her
foot. He watched her run, barefoot and in tears,
into the night. Still carrying the slipper, he turned
and walked back into the palace.

Cinderella arrived home, and waited for the others.

They were full of the things they had seen, and told her time and time again of the beautiful princess who had kept the prince talking and dancing, but who had suddenly disappeared on the stroke of midnight.

The very next day, the king and queen invited all the townspeople to the palace gates. A footman held up the glass slipper Cinderella had left behind. "The prince would like to meet whoever fits this," he announced, "for further talking and dancing."

All the women lined up to try on the shoe, but it did not fit a single one.

Finally, only Cinderella was left.
The prince was amazed
when her foot fitted the slipper
perfectly, and even more
astonished when she pulled
the other shoe out of her pocket!

"I'm not a real princess with a beautiful ballgown," admitted Cinderella, "and I don't really have a coach and footmen."
"It doesn't matter," replied the prince.
"As long as you can talk and dance like last night, we'll have lots of fun together!"